dick bruna

miffy and the new baby

EGMONT

Mother and father bunny

have some special news to tell.

And one spring day they think it's time

that Miffy knows as well.

"Hurray!" cries Miffy, dancing around.

"You've made me very happy!"

For they had said there soon would be

a little baby bunny.

“I’ll make a picture now,” she thinks,

“as pretty as can be,

a picture of some little chicks

for baby bunny to see.”

So Miffy makes a picture,

with eight small chicks in all.

And father bunny makes a frame

and hangs it on the wall.

Then mother finds a ball of wool,

would Miffy like that, too?

“Oh yes,” says Miffy, “good idea,

I’ll make a mouse in blue!”

So Miffy makes a woolly mouse,

her grandma would be proud,

for woolly mouse looks really good,

he stands out from the crowd.

Then mother bunny has her hand

upon her tummy one day,

she says, “I think this baby bunny

is almost on its way.”

And sure enough, soon after that

the time comes really fast,

and Miffy's father tells her,

"Baby bunny's here at last!"

There, in the middle of the bed,

baby bunny is safe and warm,

mother bunny looks so pleased.

She'll keep this baby safe from harm.

Miffy stands beside the bed

and thinks how very small,

that it would be so tiny

she did not know at all.

And Miffy is allowed to hold

the baby on her knee.

She feels so very grown-up now

and proud as proud can be.

The next day, Miffy takes to school

a most delicious cake

to share with all her special friends,

so all can celebrate!

miffy's library

miffy
miffy's dream
miffy goes to stay
miffy is crying
miffy at the seaside
miffy at school
miffy at the playground
miffy in hospital
miffy's bicycle
miffy at the gallery
miffy's birthday
miffy the fairy
miffy's garden
miffy and the new baby
dear grandma bunny
miffy at the zoo

miffy and the new baby
"kleine pluis"
First published in Great Britain 2005 by Egmont UK Limited
239 Kensington High Street, London W8 6SA.
Publication licensed by Mercis Publishing bv, Amsterdam

Printed in China

ISBN 978 1 4052 1903 7
10 9 8 7 6 5 4 3